D1588689

1
- 2

2

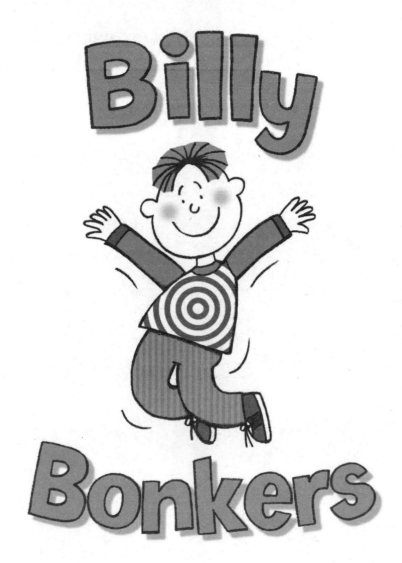

For Jacob, Jonah, Moby and Fitz
G.A.

For Jimmy Symonds
N.S.

ORCHARD BOOKS
96 Leonard Street
London EC2A 4XD
Orchard Books Australia
Hachette Children's Books
Level 17-207 Kent Street, Sydney, NSW 2000, Australia

First published in Great Britain in 2005
First paperback publication in 2006

A CIP catalogue record for this book is available from the British Library.

ISBN 1 84362 418 4 (hardback)
ISBN 1 84616 151 7 (paperback)

1 3 5 7 9 10 8 6 4 2 (hardback)
1 3 5 7 9 10 8 6 4 2 (paperback)

Printed in Great Britain

www.orchardbooks.co.uk

Billy
Bonkers

Giles Andreae
Illustrated by Nick Sharratt

ORCHARD BOOKS

Giles Andreae is an award-winning
children's author who has written many
bestselling picture books, including
Giraffes Can't Dance and *Commotion in the Ocean*.
He is probably most famous as the creator of
the phenomenally successful Purple Ronnie,
Britain's favourite stickman. Giles lives in
London and Cornwall with his wife
and three young children.

Nick Sharratt studied art at
St Martin's School of Art and has been
drawing for as long as he can remember.
He has written and illustrated many books
for children and won numerous awards
for his work. Nick lives in Brighton.

Contents

Billy Bonkers

and the
Great Porridge Incident

William Benedict Bertwhistle Bonkers was not a greedy boy. He was what his mother liked to call a hungry boy. Whatever he was or wasn't called, the one thing that was for certain was that William – or Billy as he was more commonly known – liked his food.

And there was no meal that Billy looked forward to more than breakfast. After all, there are usually only a few hours between each meal during the day, but there are a whole twelve hours that you have to get through at night without eating anything at all.

Anyway, the morning of this story, Billy bounced out of bed feeling particularly hungry. He ran downstairs in his pyjamas and found his dad reading the morning paper.

The Great Porridge Incident

"Look, Billy," said Mr Bonkers. "There are thieves in town. They're stealing everything from the local shops. Honestly, I don't know what the world is coming to," he grumbled. "It's gone mad. The world's gone mad."

This was one of Billy's dad's favourite grumbles. This and "There's so much noise in here I can't even hear myself think!" But he hadn't got to this grumble yet as he only used it in moments of panic and, so far today, there had been nothing to panic about.

***

"Don't even think about it!" Mrs Bonkers said to Billy's dad as she came downstairs in her dressing gown. Billy's dad was now looking at the adverts for sports cars in the back of his newspaper.

"Morning Billy!" said Mrs Bonkers. Then, "Look at all this washing! I sometimes think I will die under a huge pile of washing and no one will find me for weeks, by which time I'll have gone all nasty and smelly and…"

"We'll have to do the washing all over again!" said Betty Bonkers, Billy's older sister, as she came down the stairs and into the kitchen.

The Great Porridge Incident

"Very good!" said Billy's dad. "Very good!" And he laughed rather longer than he ought to have done.

"Here, I'll help you hang it out," Betty said, picking up a pair of Mrs Bonkers's enormous pants from the floor and putting them into the laundry basket.

Mrs Bonkers scowled at her husband and followed Betty outside into the garden.

***

"Right. Breakfast!" thought Billy.

His two favourite things to eat of all time (except for cake, sweets,

ice cream and chocolate)

were pork pies and porridge.

As it was breakfast, and as Mrs Bonkers's pork pies were always famously hard and overcooked, Billy thought that porridge might be more suitable – to start with anyway.

So he took the box of porridge oats out of the cupboard and poured an enormous amount of them into his favourite bowl. It was his favourite bowl not because he had made and painted it himself (although he had), not because it had a picture on it of a monster doing a poo (although it had) – by the way, he told his mum that it was a monster about to sit on a mushroom – but because it was huge. Really huge.

Now, whereas you or I would probably make our porridge with milk and heat it up a bit, Billy liked his porridge cold and with no milk in it at all. I don't know why, but that is how he liked it – straight from the packet.

"Right!" said Mrs Bonkers, coming in from the washing line. "Are you hungry today, Billy?"

"Mmmmhh, yesh," said Billy, his cheeks full of porridge, "wewy hungwy."

"Then I'll make you a nice pork pie as you were so good yesterday. A huge pork pie!"

"Shank 'ou!" said Billy, delighted, and he filled up his bowl with another enormous helping of porridge oats, and another, and another. In fact, on this particular day, Billy filled up his bowl more times than he had ever done before.

***

As Billy continued to eat his porridge his tummy began to get a little bit uncomfortable. He wriggled about on his chair and ate some more.

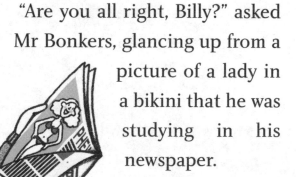

"Are you all right, Billy?" asked Mr Bonkers, glancing up from a picture of a lady in a bikini that he was studying in his newspaper.

Billy nodded his head and carried on eating.

By now, Billy's tummy was really very uncomfortable. You see, when you put milk (or any other liquid for that matter) into porridge and heat it up, the porridge swells. It absorbs the milk and gets bigger. When it gets bigger it also lets out air, which you can see as little bubbles in the saucepan.

MILK

Porridge

Air bubbles

Porridge expands

Billy, as you may remember, was eating his porridge cold and with no milk. But the inside of Billy's tummy was wet and warm. When the cold dry porridge arrived on the inside of Billy's warm wet tummy it began to swell. It swelled and swelled.

And as it swelled, it let out air. This air began to pump Billy up just like a balloon.

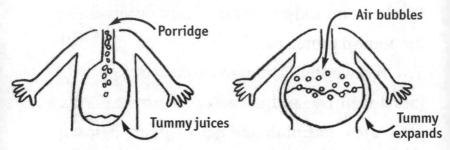

"Billy, are you really all right?" said Mr Bonkers, who still hadn't turned the page of his newspaper.

Billy nodded and ate another mouthful, but his face had gone a strange shade of green and his stomach was getting bigger by the second. Then a very peculiar thing happened. Without doing anything at all, Billy started rising off his chair.

"Piglet!" called Mr Bonkers to his wife (he didn't call her by her name, although it was Marjorie, and quite an all right name in Billy's opinion). "Piglet! Look at Billy. He's floating!"

The Great Porridge Incident

Mrs Bonkers looked up from the cooker, shrieked and ran to Mr Bonkers's side. Mr Bonkers quickly turned over the page of his newspaper.

"Oh my golly!" yelled Mrs Bonkers. "Lordy lorks! Call the police! No, the fire brigade! No, the ambulance! Oh, Sausage, who should we call? What should we do?"

Sausage was what Mrs Bonkers called her husband. This was understandable to Billy as his real name was Nigel.

At this point, Betty came into the kitchen and started yelling too.

"Be quiet!" shouted Mr Bonkers. "There's so much noise in here I can't even hear myself think!"

So everyone was quiet and watched Mr Bonkers think. Billy had now floated right off his chair and was hovering above the kitchen table.

"Oh, Piglet," wailed Mrs Bonkers again. "Whatever should we do?"

"I've absolutely no idea!" said Mr Bonkers. And then he screamed too.

***

Billy was now squashed against the kitchen ceiling, which was the only thing keeping him from floating right out of the house.

But his tummy was still swelling and swelling and it wasn't long before Billy

The Great Porridge Incident

rocketed from the kitchen, straight through the floor of Betty's bedroom. Then he splatted onto her ceiling, taking with him a pair of her pants on his head as he went.

As all the Bonkers watched through the hole in the kitchen ceiling, the inevitable happened. The roof of the house gave way, and Billy shot up and out into the bright blue sky.

The Great Porridge Incident

Before long, quite a number of people had gathered outside the Bonkers's house. They were pointing at Billy as he floated around above them.

Luckily for Billy (and *unluckily* for Billy as well – depending on how you see it), his pyjama bottoms had got caught on a branch of a tree as he floated up into the sky.

They had unravelled bit by bit until all that was left of them was a very long thread, which Billy tied to the end of his big toe to stop himself from floating away completely.

This was the reason why he now took his sister's pants off his head and put them onto his bottom. It was the only time in his whole life that he would be happy wearing a pair of pants with flowers and frilly bits on them.

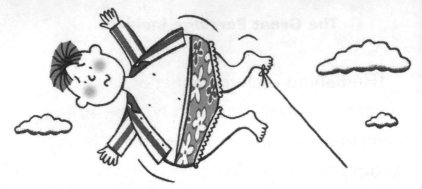

The trouble was that there was Billy, bobbing about in the sky like a giant balloon on a string, but nobody had any idea how to get him down.

"Let's get a ladder!" suggested one man.

But no one had a ladder, not even the fire brigade, that was anything like long enough.

The Great Porridge Incident

"How about an aeroplane
or a helicopter?" said
someone else. But no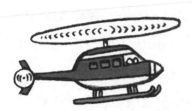
aeroplane or helicopter would have

been able to get close
enough to the tree.

Then a lady came along pushing a pram.
"Whatever is the matter?" she said to
Betty, picking up her
baby and patting him
on the back.

"It's my brother Billy," said Betty Bonkers. "That's him up there in my pants."

"However did that happen?" said the lady.

"Well, he ate cold dry porridge, which swelled up inside him and he floated off his chair and burst through the kitchen ceiling and my bedroom ceiling and his pyjamas got stuck on the tree and he had my pants on his head so… WAIT A MINUTE!" Betty shouted, as the baby did a little burp. "I think I might have an idea!"

The baby burped again and began to gurgle happily.

"That's it!" said Betty. "I've got it!"

"You've got what?" said the lady.

"Your baby just burped!" said Betty. "That's what Billy needs to do. When a baby is full of wind, he needs to burp. Don't you see? Billy's full of wind. BILLY NEEDS TO BURP!"

Everybody agreed that this was probably right. It was worth a try, at least. So Betty Bonkers shouted up to her brother, "Billy! You need to burp! That porridge has filled you full of air – you need to burp!"

Now, some people are able to do a burp just like that. They have a special way in which they can take a little gulp of air and let out a great belch a moment afterwards. Sadly, Billy was not one of those people, although he had often wished that he was. Never had he wished this more than right now.

He tried to suck and gulp and swallow all at the same time, but it just seemed to make him even fatter and more full of air than ever before.

After a while he stopped. "I can't!" he shouted. "It's no use! I can't burp!"

"But you have to!" shouted Betty. "It's the only way we're going to be able to get you down!"

But Billy knew that if you don't know how to burp, you don't know how to burp and that was that.

Then Betty had another thought. "Hang on!" she said. "We need to pat him. That's

what you do to a baby when you can't get a
baby to burp. You pat him on the back!"

"How on earth do we pat
him on the back?" said
Mr Bonkers. "He's
miles away up in
the air!"

Betty thought.
"Mum," she said.
"Is that pork pie of
yours still in the oven?"

"Oh, lordy lorks!" said
Mrs Bonkers. "In all
the commotion I've
overcooked it again!"

"That's great!" said
Betty. "It'll be perfect!"

"No, it won't," said
Mrs Bonkers. "It'll
be ruined!"

"No!" said Betty. "You see, we need it nice and hard for Billy. If we can hit him on the back with something hard then it might just get him to burp!"

"I see!" said Mrs Bonkers, pleased for once that the hardness of her pork pies was going to be a thing of usefulness rather than a joke.

"But how on earth do we ever hit him with a pork pie?" said Mr Bonkers. "No one can throw anything that far, let alone a giant overcooked pork pie. It's mad! You're all mad! The world's gone mad!"

"Mum's pants!" said Betty. "We'll use Mum's pants as a catapult!"

Now, I have mentioned before that Mrs Bonkers's pants were enormous. This was a funny thing, as Mrs Bonkers herself was not enormous. She just liked to wear enormous pants. They felt comfortable and, as she often told her husband, she was allowed to because she was a mummy.

"We'll stretch out a pair of Mum's pants between these two trees, and we'll fire the pork pie from the pants straight at Billy!" said Betty Bonkers.

"But you'll ruin my pants!" said Mrs Bonkers.

"Never mind. I'll buy you another pair," said Mr Bonkers eagerly, thinking of the lady in the bikini from his newspaper.

"OK," said Billy's mum. "He is my son, after all!"

So Betty took the biggest pair of pants that she could find off the washing line, and stretched them out between two trees in the front garden.

She took the giant pork pie out of the oven (it was very hard and almost black by now) and placed it inside the pants. She pulled back the pants and everyone stood in silence, waiting to see what would happen.

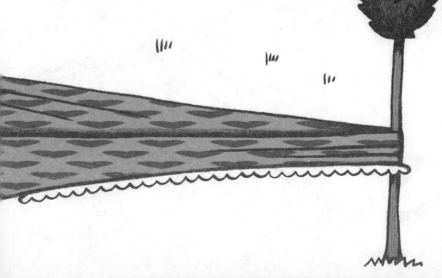

"THREE…TWO…ONE…" said Billy's dad. "FIRE!"

Betty let go of the pants, and the pork pie came shooting out as fast as a rocket. It flew up into the air and, to everyone's astonishment, it hit Billy slap bang in the middle of his back.

There was a small pause. Then Billy felt
his tummy begin to turn around and
around like a washing machine. It churned
and wobbled and rumbled and then it
happened…

Billy did the most enormous burp the world has ever known.

The Great Porridge Incident

I don't really know how to spell a burp such as this. I couldn't get anywhere near to imitating the sound, but I hope you can imagine the kind of burp that this was. It was the kind of burp that shook houses and that blew birds out of trees.

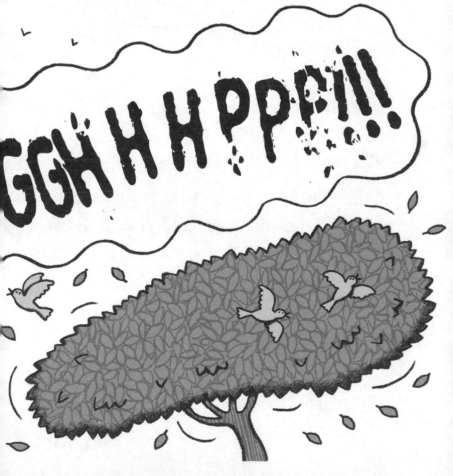

The piece of thread tied around Billy's toe that used to be his pyjamas instantly snapped in two and Billy went shooting off into the air.

When you blow up a balloon and then let it go without tying a knot at the bottom, it goes flying around all over the place, looping and twisting and making figures-of-eight in the air. And this is exactly what happened to Billy. The air was escaping from him just like it would from a balloon,

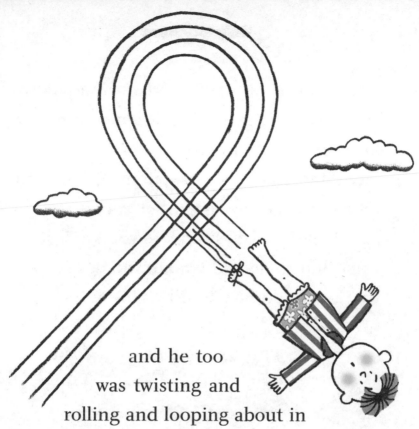

and he too
was twisting and
rolling and looping about in
the sky in really quite a graceful manner.

Suddenly he came blasting down towards the ground. He hovered above it for a second and then shot off along the street, with the assembled crowd running along behind him.

***

Now, because of this great commotion, everybody in the whole town had come out to see what was going on. Everybody including all the shopkeepers. This meant that it was an ideal time for robbers to go about their business and, as you know from what Billy's dad had read in the newspaper, there were robbers in Billy's town.

The Great Porridge Incident

Little did the robbers know what was about to happen to them as, at that very moment, they broke into Mrs Dingleberry's Cake, Sweets, Chocolate and Ice Cream Emporium and took all the money in the till, all the cakes in the fridge, all the sweets on the shelves, all the chocolates in the counter and all the ice cream in the freezer.

Billy Bonkers

Not in their wildest dreams could they have imagined that a boy, wearing hardly anything at all except for his sister's frilly pants, would come hurtling towards them at a hundred miles an hour a few inches above the ground and slam right into them, knocking them over as they were trying to escape, and sending money, cakes, sweets, chocolates and ice cream flying about in all directions.

But this is
exactly what
happened.

And as Billy picked himself up off the ground, the police (who had also been watching this extraordinary event) came running over and slapped the robbers into handcuffs.

"Well done, Billy!" said the chief policeman. "We've been looking for this gang of villains for a long time and you've caught them all at once – single-handed! You deserve a great big medal and we'll make sure that you get one!"

Mr and Mrs Bonkers, who had now caught up with Billy, threw their arms around him.

"Lordy lorks!" cried Mrs Bonkers. "You're safe, Billy! You're safe!" She was weeping with joy.

The Great Porridge Incident

"Is this your son?" said the policeman to Mr Bonkers.

"Yes, he is!" replied Betty. "And he's my brother too!"

"Well," said the policeman, "you ought to be extremely proud of him. He's a very brave chap indeed. In fact, he's a hero."

Everyone in the whole crowd cheered and clapped. "You're a hero!" they shouted. "Billy's a hero!"

Mrs Dingleberry was so pleased with what Billy had done that she said he could have free cake, sweets, chocolates and ice cream from her Emporium as often as he wanted for the whole of the rest of his life!

The Great Porridge Incident

Billy was very pleased indeed. He was so pleased in fact that, as the crowd lifted him up onto their shoulders and paraded him through the town, he forgot, just for a moment, that he was still wearing his sister's frilly pants.

THE END

Billy Bonkers

and the
Great Beach Rescue

It was the first day of the annual Bonkers's summer holiday!

Mr and Mrs Bonkers, Billy and Betty were walking down the path from the car park to the beach. They were piled high with practically everything from their house that could possibly be squished into one car.

There were windbreaks, Lilos, buckets and spades, sandwiches, drinks, suncreams,

sweaters, footpumps, swimming costumes, tennis rackets, surfboards, beach balls, wetsuits, hats…and if I keep on listing everything they were carrying I'll fill up all the pages in this book before I've even got to the beginning of this story! Let's just say they were carrying a lot of stuff.

"I think just here would be good," said Mr Bonkers, scanning the beach from behind

his sunglasses. "Yes, just about exactly here is perfect!"

Betty dumped her rug on the beach and spread it out over the sand.

"Phew!" panted Billy, collapsing on top of it, sweat pouring from his face which had turned the colour of a sunburnt tomato.

"Just what are you looking at?" said Mrs Bonkers to her husband.

"Oh, um, nothing, Piglet," said Mr Bonkers. Piglet was what Mr Bonkers called his wife when he was trying not to get into trouble. "Just, um…looking around really. Lovely day!"

"They are almost half your age, Nigel Bonkers, and you are a married man," said Billy's mum, looking at the group of girls playing volleyball in their bikinis right next to the place where her husband had chosen to set up their camp. "Is that why you chose this spot, by any chance?"

"Good lord, no. Hadn't even noticed them!" said Mr Bonkers, his face turning the same colour as Billy's. "Goodness, look at those swimming costumes! What is the world coming to? It's gone mad! The world's gone mad!"

"You can stop looking at those swimming costumes now," said Mrs Bonkers, "and help us to get everything sorted. Betty, you unpack the toys and the picnic. Billy, you blow up the Lilo with this pump, please, and Sausage, you can set up the windbreak." Sausage was what Mrs Bonkers called her husband when she wasn't telling him off.

Mr Bonkers picked up the mallet and started knocking the posts of the windbreak in one by one.

"Sausage, you don't need to bash them quite so hard," said Mrs Bonkers. "You're trying to impress those girls, aren't you?"

"What girls?" said Mr Bonkers, trying to look innocent. "Oh, *those* girls!" He laughed. "Yes, I'd forgotten they were even there!"

"Then you can stop pulling your tummy in and come and rub some suncream onto my back," said his wife.

Mr Bonkers did as he was told.

"Excuse me," said a voice. "Do you mind if I get my ball?"

Billy looked up. It was one of the bikini girls.

"Oh, I see you've got a pump!" the girl said to him. "Could we possibly use it to put a bit of air into our ball? It's gone rather flat."

"Yes, yes, of course

you can, can't they, Billy?" said Mr Bonkers, springing to his feet. "In fact, here, let me do it for you!"

Billy handed the pump to his dad.

"Oh, and a surfboard!" said the girl. "Cool! I'm going to learn this year. Do you surf?" she said to Mr Bonkers.

"Er, it's Billy's," said Mr Bonkers. "Billy and Betty surf. Of course I used to…taught them everything they know. Carving, um, sliding, hanging ten, you know, that sort of thing. Can't really be bothered any more. Prefer to just, you know…chill out."

"Dad…" said Betty, trying to catch his attention.

"You know there's a surfing competition on the beach today," said the girl. "Why don't you sign up? Get a bit of practice in again. You sound good!"

"Yes, well, maybe another day," said Mr Bonkers.

Mrs Bonkers wondered whether to tell the girl that her husband hadn't even learnt to swim, but she thought better of it.

"Dad…" said Betty again. "Dad…"
Suddenly there was an enormous

Mr Bonkers, whose eyes had not been trained on the volleyball at any time while he was blowing it up, had pumped so much air into it that it exploded on the end of the pump and shot off along the beach.

"Um, that's what I was trying to tell you," said Betty, helpfully.

The Great Beach Rescue

"Oh, I'm so sorry!" said Mr Bonkers to the girl. "I was looking at your...well, I...hey! Why don't you use our ball?" he said quickly. "You can use our beach ball, can't they children?"

"OK," said Billy.

"Why don't you guys come and play with us?" the girl said to Billy and Betty. "We could use some more players!"

"Yeah," said Billy. "That would be cool!"

So Billy and Betty began playing volleyball with the bikini girls. The girls were very good. They were a lot older than

Billy and Betty and a lot taller too, so Billy and Betty had to play their absolute best.

"I'll show them how good I can be!" thought Billy when it was his serve. He picked up the beach ball, threw it in the air, and gave it an almighty whack with his fist.

Oomph!

The ball was so light that it flew up and up into the air and then got caught by a strong gust of wind. It veered sideways, landed on the wet sand by the water and rolled towards the sea. Just then, a big wave came along and swept the ball out into the ocean with it.

In no time at all, the ball had become just a small dot in the distance.

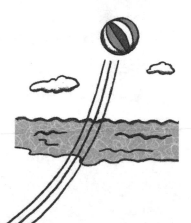

"Oh, no!" shouted Billy. "I'm really sorry. Don't worry, I'll get it!"

"No, you can't!" said the bikini girl.

"You're too young to swim that far." She looked at Mr Bonkers expectantly.

"What?" he said. "Oh, yes, um, well, I'd better swim out and…ow, my leg!" he yelled, clutching his ankle. "Old surfing injury playing up!"

Mr Bonkers began hopping from foot to foot.

"Oh, I'll get it, then," said the bikini girl. She grabbed Billy's surfboard and began to paddle out towards the beach ball.

Everybody watched her. She paddled and paddled, but the ball was getting carried further and further away from the beach and out to sea.

Then, in the distance, an enormous wave began to appear. A wave bigger than Billy or Betty or Mr Bonkers or Mrs Bonkers or any of the other bikini girls had ever seen before. It was colossal. And it was building and building.

But, even worse than that, just in front of the wave, Billy thought that he could see a grey fin carving through the surface of the water, heading straight towards the bikini girl on his surfboard. The grey fin...of a great white shark!

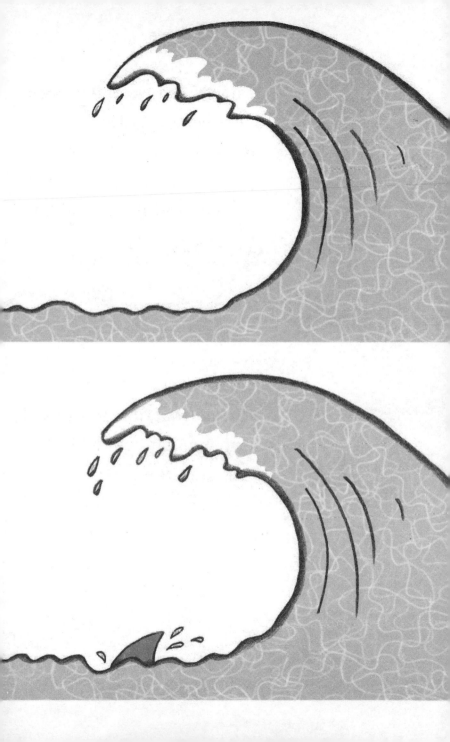

The bikini girl looked up and saw both the enormous wave and the sharp grey fin at exactly the same time.

AAAaaaaahhhhh!

she yelled.

SHARK! HEEEEELP!

Instantly, there was panic. Nobody knew what to do. "She's too far out!" yelled the bikini girl's friends. "None of us can swim that far! She's going to die!"

"Oh lordy, lordy lorks!" wailed Mrs Bonkers. "I knew we'd forget something! I knew it! If only we'd brought the puncture repair kit, they'd never have had to use the beach ball and…"

"Be quiet!" shouted Mr Bonkers. "There's so much noise I can't even hear myself think!"

"Wait," shouted Betty, who was watching a family on the beach not far away. "I think I might have an idea!"

The mother was watching her little children play as she was blowing up a pair of armbands.

"Look, Billy," said Betty, pointing, "what are *they?*"

"They're armbands," said Billy. "But I don't need armbands. I can swim! I just can't swim that far!"

"They're armbands..." said Betty, "...or JET-PROPELLED ROCKET BOOSTERS!"

"Jet-propelled what?" said Billy.

"Jet-propelled rocket boosters!" said Betty again. "You know how Dad pumped that volleyball up so hard that it got bigger and bigger and bigger until it couldn't get any bigger any more so it burst and shot along the ground?"

"Yes..." said Billy.

"Well, that's what we could do with those armbands!" said Betty. "We could put them on your arms and blow them up and up and up until they're just about ready to burst..."

"Yes..." said Billy, beginning to see what Betty might be getting at.

"And then we could get a couple of those little kebab sticks from Mum's picnic and just make a tiny prick in each of the armbands. They should have enough pressure in them to lift you off the ground and, if you're pointing in the right direction, to blast you over to that girl!"

"Then what?" said Billy's mum. "How does he get back?"

"Never mind 'then what'!" said Billy. "It's the only choice we have!" He ran over to the lady with the armbands. "Emergency!" he said. "I need to borrow your armbands to save a girl's life! May I?"

"Well, of course!" said the lady, and she gave Billy the armbands.

"Quick!" said Billy to his dad. "Get the pump!"

Mr Bonkers did as he was told and, as fast as he could, he pumped and pumped and pumped. The armbands got bigger and bigger and bigger until finally Betty shouted, "Stop! That should be enough! Mum, get the kebab sticks!"

The Great Beach Rescue

Mrs Bonkers hurried over with two kebab sticks and Betty held one gently against each armband.

"Are you ready, Billy?" she said.

Billy gulped. He leaned forward a bit and held his arms tight against his sides like he had seen ski jumpers do on TV.

"Ready!" he said.

"Right," said Betty. "Three…two…one…"
Everyone held their breath.

"Blast off!"

shouted Betty, stabbing the bottom of each
armband hard with the kebab sticks.

There was a loud

and, before anyone was able to say anything
at all, Billy had rocketed into the air and
was flying at several hundred miles an hour
through the sky towards the bikini girl.

He looked down and saw her waving her arms and shouting. "HELP! HELP! HELP!"

"Don't worry!" shouted Billy. "I'm coming!" But the shark was getting closer and closer and the huge wave wasn't far away now either.

By moving his head slightly and tilting his shoulders, Billy found that he could change the direction of his flight. This is what he did now to start his descent towards the shark.

"HELP!" shouted the girl. "It's going to get me! I'm going to be a shark sandwich!"

And it was true. Billy was just too far away. He saw the shark opening its huge jaws. It was only a few feet away from the girl now.

In a final attempt to gather speed, Billy tucked his neck into his shoulders, closed his eyes, clenched his fists and pointed his toes…

SpLAAAATTT!

I don't know exactly what noise a boy's head makes when it collides at several hundred miles an hour with the nose of a shark, but it's something pretty much like **SPLAT!** anyway.

Yes – at the very moment when the shark was about to bring its jaws chomping down around the helpless bikini girl's middle, Billy had crunched with all his might into the poor shark's nose. I say poor shark not because I like sharks, but because anyone whose nose is crunched into by a boy flying quite as fast as Billy happened to be flying deserves as much sympathy as they can get.

And if you know anything about sharks, you will know that the only place that sharks don't like to be hit is on their noses. If you hit a shark hard enough on the end of its nose, you will stun it, and this is exactly what happened to the poor shark that Billy crashed into. It was totally and utterly stunned. So stunned, in fact, that when it finally came to its senses again, it had entirely forgotten that it was a shark and ended up giving children rides from

the beach, but that is another story altogether.

"Oh, Billy!" said the bikini girl. "Billy, you've saved me! You're my hero!"

"Not so fast!" said Billy, looking up. Sure enough, right behind them, was the most enormous wave that Billy had ever seen. It was a wave of quite terrifying proportions.

"Can you ride it?" asked the bikini girl.

"Are you joking?" said Billy. "I've only had one lesson! Not even a pro could ride that monster!" He paused. "But we've got no choice," he said. "I'm going to have to. Hold tight! Hold very tight!"

So the bikini girl held onto Billy, and Billy slid onto his surfboard. The wave was towering behind him. It was as big as a house. Bigger. Billy began to paddle. He paddled and paddled, quicker and quicker, until he felt the wave rising behind him.

"Faster! Faster!" he said to himself. Then he felt a sudden surge of speed beneath him and quickly, smoothly he leapt to his feet.

He was standing! He was actually standing! And, best of all, the bikini girl was standing on the board behind him too, her arms clinging, for all she was worth, around his waist.

"Wowee!" yelled Billy. "We've caught it! We're riding the wave! We're actually riding the monster wave of all time!"

Billy carved and spun and glided all the way to the shore before casually flipping out of the wave just before it crashed onto the sand, soaking all of the people on the beach. But they didn't mind. Everybody on the beach was cheering and waving and clapping and shouting Billy's name!

"BILLY! BILLY! BILLY'S A HERO!" was all he could hear.

The bikini girl gave Billy a huge kiss, which made him go bright red (for the second time that day). "You saved my life!" she said, breathlessly. "How can I ever thank you?"

"It was nothing really," said Billy, smiling. "I guess I just did what I had to."

But that was not what the bikini girl's friends thought as they lifted him onto their shoulders and paraded him along the beach.

And that was not what the brown man with big muscles, a flat tummy and baggy shorts thought as he caught up with Billy. "You've done it, mate," he said. "No one else would have dared go near that cahoona, but you took it all the way to the beach!

The Great Beach Rescue

Awesome! Totally radical and awesome! I'm the winner of last year's surfing competition and the judge of this year's. You've won it hands down! No competition! Congratulations, mate! What's your name?"

"Bonkers," said Billy. "Billy Bonkers. What surfing competition?" he asked.

"This one!" said the judge, thrusting a huge silver cup into Billy's hands. "World Champion" it said on the side.

"Wow!" said Billy.

"That's my son!" shouted Mr Bonkers proudly to anyone who would listen. "On those girls' shoulders! That's my son!"

"And as for you, young lady," said the surfing competition judge to Betty, "I couldn't help noticing what part you played in this whole fiasco. You're a pretty clever girl."

Then he turned to Mrs Bonkers. "Sister or mother?" he said.

Mrs Bonkers let out a strange giggle and went a brighter shade of scarlet than anyone else had that day.

The Great Beach Rescue

"Look, Billy," said the judge, "there's a party on the beach tonight. Since you're our new champion, you must come along and bring all your family with you as our guests of honour!"

"Wow, thanks!" said Billy, still clutching his cup. "That would be great!"

"Hey, don't thank *me*," said the judge. "I want to thank *you* for doing what you did today. I tell you, those girls aren't the only people around here who think you're a hero. In fact, mate, you're not just a hero..." he said, putting his arm around Billy's shoulder and smiling, "... you're a *legend*!"

THE END

Billy
Bonkers

and the
Birthday Trampoline

"Hooray! It's my birthday!" Billy Bonkers said to himself as he bounced out of bed. "I wonder what present Mum and Dad have got for me this year?"

Last year, Mr and Mrs Bonkers had given Billy an enormous super-powered telescope. It was so big that it had to sit on its own special stand, and it was so powerful that when Billy first looked through it he was sure that he could actually see the footsteps of the men who had landed on the moon.

He could also see a smaller planet right next to the moon, which looked as though it was made entirely of chocolate. He never told anyone about this planet because, one day, Billy planned to become an astronaut himself and be the very first person to land there.

Planet Billy, he would call it. Only he would be allowed to go there, since he had discovered it, and he would bring back little bits  of space chocolate and sell them for loads of money to millionaires all over the world.

Anyway, this year Billy bounded down the stairs into the kitchen to be greeted by…

Hurry up, Billy!

It was Mrs Bonkers. Or at least it was the voice of Mrs Bonkers. She had such an enormous pile of washing in her arms that she looked more like a great headless ball of walking clothes, with only a pair of pink fluffy slippers for feet.

"Come on, Billy. We'll be late for school," added Mr Bonkers, from behind his newspaper. "Good lord, the rubbish they put in the papers these days. The world's gone mad!"

Billy couldn't believe it. Not a mention of "Happy birthday, Billy!" And not a present in sight.

Suddenly, there was a rumpus at the top of the stairs. "Who's got my hairbrush? Where's my hairbrush?" It was Betty. Betty hated getting out of bed and, as a result, was always late for school.

"I don't know where your silly hairbrush is," said Billy, "and I don't care because today it's my b—"

"Billy!" shouted Betty. She ran down the stairs with her arms outstretched. "Happy b—"

"Ahem!" coughed Mr Bonkers, so loudly that he even frightened himself a bit.

"Oh, yes, sorry," said Betty. "Uh, morning, Billy," she said, and kissed him on the cheek.

"Porridge!" shouted Mrs Bonkers, putting down Billy's favourite bowl on the table in front of him. Billy always had milk in his porridge now, for reasons which I imagine you already know.

"Right," said Mr Bonkers, putting down his newspaper. "School!"

Billy was so upset he didn't know what to do. Nobody in his whole family, not one person, had remembered his birthday.

He finished his porridge, grabbed his lunchbox and stomped out of the kitchen door into the garden. "Nobody!" he muttered to himself. "Not Mum, not Dad, not even Betty. It's so unfair! It's SO UNF—"

Suddenly Billy stopped. There, in front of him, was the biggest, hugest, enormousest trampoline that Billy had ever seen in his life.

"SURPRISE!" shouted Mr and Mrs Bonkers and Betty, who were all now laughing in the doorway behind him. "Happy birthday, Billy!"

"Wow!" said Billy. "Oh, wowee! It's amazing!"

Now Billy, as you know, was a very bouncy boy, so an enormous trampoline was about the best thing that anyone could possibly have given him in the whole world.

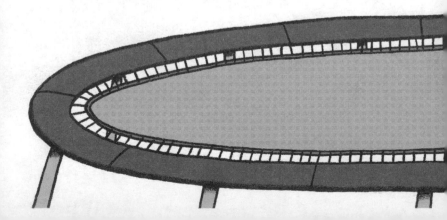

The Birthday Trampoline

"Can I get on it?" asked Billy, almost bursting with excitement.

"You'll be late for school," said Mrs Bonkers, smiling.

"Who cares about school when there's bouncing to be done!" said Mr Bonkers. "Go on, Billy, show us what you can do!"

So Billy climbed onto the trampoline and began to bounce. Higher and higher he went until he was bouncing nearly as high as the roof of his house.

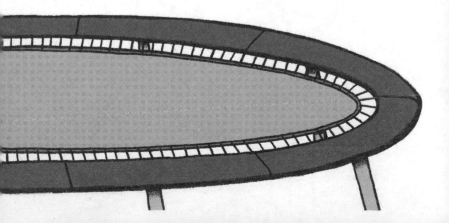

"You can go higher than that!" said Mr Bonkers, pulling off his shoes and climbing onto the trampoline. "Here, I'll show you how it's done!"

First Billy bounced, then Mr Bonkers bounced. Then Billy bounced and Mr Bonkers bounced again.

Soon they were both bouncing together in really quite a graceful rhythm, getting higher and higher as they did so.

Then Mr Bonkers did an unbelievably enormous bounce and, when he came down, he hit the trampoline at exactly the same time as Billy.

Now, I don't know if you've ever bounced on a trampoline with a grown-up but, if you have, you'll know that if you both bounce at exactly the same time, a funny thing happens. You bounce a lot higher, and I mean a LOT higher, than you do if you are just bouncing on your own.

So when Mr Bonkers landed on the mat with Billy right beside him…

...SPROING!!!!

Billy went shooting up into the air about as quickly as an exploding missile. Up and up he went, past the houses, past the trees and past the birds.

"He's not stopping!" shouted Betty. "What's happening? When's he going to come down?"

But Billy was not going to come down. You see, that bounce was a bigger bounce than anyone had ever done before in the history of the universe. Billy was soaring up into space and Billy was going to carry on soaring up into space…until he hit something.

"I'm flying!" yelled Billy, his cheeks flapping in the wind and his hair blasted flat against his head. "I'm really flyyyyiiing"

PPFFTHLLRRGGHHH!!!

That was meant to be an enormous squelchy noise – a bit like an enormous squelchy fart. If you are reading this book to yourself, why not make the noise out loud to see what it's meant to sound like. If a grown-up is reading this story to you and they didn't make it sound enough like a fart, then you have my permission to tickle them until they say "PPFFTHLLRRGGHHH!!!" properly.

PPFFTHLLRRGGHHH!!!

Billy had crashed head first right into the middle of a planet. But it was not just any planet. It was the very planet that Billy had seen from his own bedroom window through his giant telescope. And not only was the outside of the planet covered entirely with chocolate, but the inside was made up entirely of…SWEETS!

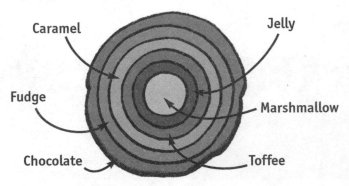

Caramel

Jelly

Fudge

Marshmallow

Chocolate

Toffee

The Birthday Trampoline

When Billy realised this, he thought to himself, "Oh well, I'll just have to munch my way out." And that is exactly what he did.

First he ate through some marshmallow, then he gobbled a layer of jelly, then he chewed through some toffee, then he slurped up some caramel, then he ate a whole layer of fudge until, finally, he munched his way through an absolutely enormous crust of chocolate.

Billy Bonkers

When Billy finally got to the surface, he stood up and looked around. There, right beside him, was a group of five extraordinary-looking green aliens. When the aliens saw Billy they knelt down at his feet. They had never seen anyone like him before, and they thought that he must have been sent to them as their new king.

"Greetings," they said. **"We worship you, O mighty one."**

"Oh, um, that's very nice," said Billy. "Thank you."

"What is your name, O king and master?" said the aliens.

"Billy Bonkers," said Billy.

"Jilly Jonkers," said the aliens who, for some reason, were quite unable to pronounce their "b"s.

"No, uh…Billy Bonkers," said Billy.

"Silly Sonkers," replied the aliens.

"No, it's…oh, never mind," said Billy. "Look, how do I get off this planet?"

"No one has ever left this planet," said the aliens. "Why would anyone want to? Please stay. Eat as much as you like."

"I can't," said Billy. "I've got to get home. It's my birthday!"

Meanwhile, back at the Bonkers's house, there was panic.

"Lordy lorks, he's gone!" wailed Mrs Bonkers. "He's gone for ever! I'm never going to see my darling Billy again! Oh, Sausage, whatever can we do?"

The Birthday Trampoline

"Calm down, Piglet," said Mr Bonkers. "There's so much noise I can't even hear myself think!"

"I know," said Betty. "Let's get Billy's telescope and see if we can find him anywhere up there in the sky."

"Good idea," said Mr Bonkers, running off to fetch it.

Betty set up the telescope and peered through it. "It's too light," she said. "I can't see anything. We're going to have to wait until it gets darker."

Billy Bonkers

So, for the rest of that day, the Bonkers family waited anxiously until it got dark and, way up in space, Billy ate and ate and ate until he was so full of sweets and chocolate that he could hardly move at all.

"It's time," announced Betty, just after tea. And she went out into the garden and began to peer through the telescope.

After a bit, something caught her eye. Up there in the sky, right next to the moon, Betty could clearly see a planet, a brownish planet, with something moving on it.

The Birthday Trampoline

At first, all she could see was a group of weird-looking green things kneeling on the ground but, when she looked harder, she was sure that they were kneeling in front of a very big, very round version of her brother...Billy!

"It's him!' she cried. "It's our Billy! He's up there in space...on a planet...surrounded by aliens!"

"Oh, Billy!" wept Mrs Bonkers. "My Billy! We must get him down at once. But how, Sausage?" she said, turning to Mr Bonkers. "How on earth do we get him down from up there?"

"I think I might have an idea!" said Betty. "We can use the *telescope* to get him down!"

"Have you gone out of your mind, Betty?" said Mr Bonkers. "We can't poke him down with a telescope. It won't reach anything like that far."

"I know," said Betty. "Of course we can't

poke him down…but we can MELT him down!"

"Melt him!" yelled Mrs Bonkers. "Melt my Billy? Oh, lordy lorks, Sausage, she's gone completely mad."

"Mad!" agreed Mr Bonkers. "The girl's gone mad!"

"No, not melt *Billy*," said Betty. "Melt the *planet*. I've had a good look through the telescope and, although it sounds quite strange I know, I'm almost certain that the planet Billy's stuck on is made of chocolate."

"What…?" said Mr Bonkers, looking at his daughter as though she was completely barmy.

"If, when the sun comes out tomorrow, we point the telescope directly at it, we can focus its rays onto a mirror and bounce back a really powerful beam of light at the planet Billy's stuck on. With any luck, that beam will be hot enough to melt a planet made of chocolate, and Billy will fall back down to Earth…simple!" she added.

The Birthday Trampoline

"Mum, you know your spot-squeezing mirror?"

"Um, you mean my make-up mirror, dear," said Mrs Bonkers.

"Yes, that one," said Betty. "That's got a sort of magnifying bit as well, hasn't it? So, if we bounce the beam of light from the telescope off your mirror back to Billy's planet, it might make it even more powerful still!"

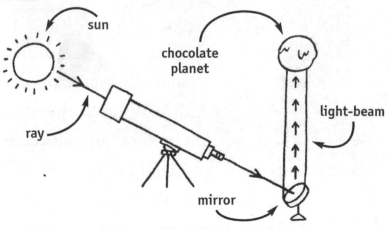

"She's crackers!" said Mr Bonkers. "Loopy as fruit cake…but it's worth a try."

That night, Mr and Mrs Bonkers stayed out in the garden all night, taking turns to peer at Billy through the giant telescope. Betty was making all sorts of calculations and charts so that, when the sun rose, she could have the telescope and the mirror set up in exactly the right positions to fire the beam of light straight at Billy's planet.

When dawn came, everything was in place. The Bonkerses waited anxiously to see what would happen.

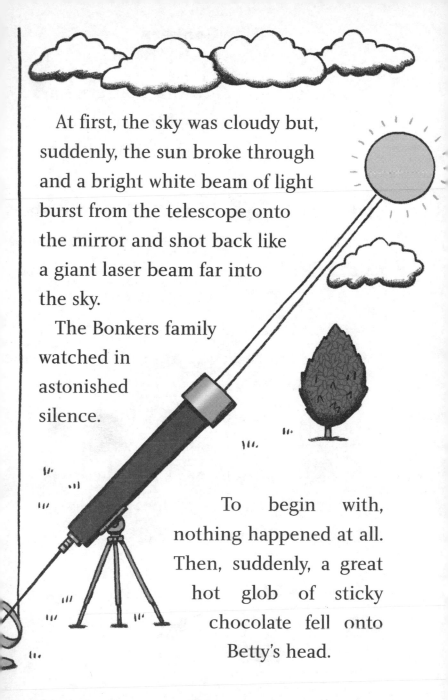

At first, the sky was cloudy but, suddenly, the sun broke through and a bright white beam of light burst from the telescope onto the mirror and shot back like a giant laser beam far into the sky.

The Bonkers family watched in astonished silence.

To begin with, nothing happened at all. Then, suddenly, a great hot glob of sticky chocolate fell onto Betty's head.

"Look!" she shouted, wiping a handful of the goo from her hair. "I think it's working!"

Gradually, more and more dollops of chocolate began to fall from the sky, and it wasn't long before the whole of the Bonkers's front garden was covered with a sticky mess of melted chocolate, jelly, caramel, marshmallow, fudge and toffee.

Then, as the Bonkerses looked up, high in the distance they could see the unmistakable shape of their son Billy tumbling and falling through the sky towards them, followed closely by a group of five aliens.

"Quick!" shouted Mr Bonkers. "Let's get the trampoline underneath him or he'll be squashed as flat as a pancake when he hits the ground!"

So they dragged the trampoline across the garden to the exact spot where it looked as if Billy was going to land.

"Oh, no!" shouted Betty. "Look! His trousers are on fire. The beam from the telescope must have hit them as well and set them alight!"

Mr and Mrs Bonkers looked up and saw plumes of smoke billowing from the back of Billy's trousers.

Then Betty had another thought. "If he lands on the trampoline, it's just going to bounce him back up into space," she said. "We're going to have to aim the trampoline *at* something – something that will give him a soft landing."

Betty thought for a moment. "I've got it!" she said. "What about the Rockets' swimming pool next door? If we lift up one side of the trampoline, we might just be able to bounce Billy over the hedge and into the Rockets' swimming pool. That will put out the fire in his trousers as well!"

"You're crazy, Betty," said Mr Bonkers. "But it might just be worth a try!"

So Mr and Mrs Bonkers heaved up one side of the trampoline until Betty said, "That's it! Keep it there! Hold steady!"

Billy was hurtling as fast as a missile back down to Earth, flames streaming from his trousers.

The Birthday Trampoline

"Here he comes," said Betty. "Three…
two…
one…"

Suddenly, Mr
and Mrs Bonkers both felt
an enormous

SpROING!

on the trampoline, followed
shortly by several more.

Billy shot off the mat,
with the aliens close
behind him, back up
into the sky.

Moments later, they could clearly hear a series of loud splashes from the garden next door.

"We've done it!" shouted Betty. "I think we've really done it! Quick, Dad, let's go and see if Billy's all right."

"Hello, Mr Rocket," said Mr Bonkers, leaping over the gate and whizzing past his neighbour. "I think my chocolate-covered

son with his pants on fire and a load of green aliens have just fallen out of the sky into your swimming pool."

Sure enough, climbing out of the Rockets' pool, his whole body covered in chocolate, was Billy. His trousers were in smoking tatters and, behind him, stood five green aliens.

"Billy!" said Mr Bonkers, hugging his son. "It's really you! You're back!"

"Yes," said Billy, licking the chocolate from his face, "and these are my new friends. They think I'm their king!"

"Greetings, Mr Conkers!" said the aliens.

"Um, yes, greetings indeed!" said Mr Bonkers. "Well, you'd better all come home with me then."

The Birthday Trampoline

"Oh, Billy," said Mrs Bonkers when they had all got back to the house. "I'm so glad that you're safe! Now, let's get those sticky clothes off you and put them straight in the wash!"

"And as for you," she said, turning to the aliens, "you all need a good scrub down. Come on! Follow me! Up to the bath!"

"Yes, Mrs Donkers," said the aliens, doing as they were told.

"Betty," whispered Mrs Bonkers over her shoulder. "Seeing as you're so clever, do you think you can work out a way of getting these aliens back up into space?"

The Birthday Trampoline

"Hmmm," said Betty. "I'll see what I can do, but Billy does seem to rather like them."

"Mum," said Billy. "Can't they stay just for a little while?"

"Oh, all right, Billy," said Mrs Bonkers, smiling. "Just for a little while. After all, it is your birthday!"

THE END